# JUNK, SWEET JUNK

ISBN 0-590-03234-8

12 11 10 9 8 7 6 5 4 3 2                    8 9/9 0 1 2/0

Printed in the U.S.A.                    23

First Scholastic printing, September 1997

# JUNK, SWEET JUNK

## by Molly Wigand
## illustrated by Barry Goldberg

SCHOLASTIC INC.

New York   Toronto   London   Auckland   Sydney

Tommy's dad, Stu, looked around his house. "There's no room in our rooms! We need a bigger house."

"No!" said Tommy's mom, Didi.
"We have too much junk. Let's have
a junk sale! Then there will be lots
of room in our house."

The junk sale was in Tommy's yard.

"I'm hot," said Angelica.

Tommy reached into a box.

"That's a bird," said Angelica. "See the feathers?"

Tommy said, "It's not a bird! It's a tummy tickler!"

"Tickle my tummy!" said Chuckie.

Tommy tickled Chuckie right on the tummy. Chuckie giggled.

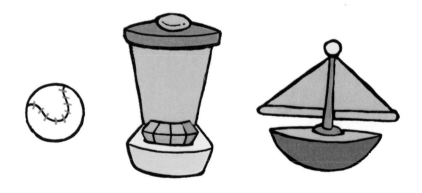

"There's something soft inside,"
said Chuckie.

Tommy reached into the box.
"Baseball pajamas! Let's play ball!"

Tommy put on the pajama top.
Chuckie put on the pajama bottom.
   Tommy pitched a ball to Angelica.
She hit it. "Home run!" she yelled.

Chuckie caught the ball.
"You're out, Angelica!" said Tommy.
Angelica was mad. "I'm out of here!"
She walked away.

Then she saw a really big box.

"There's something hard in this box," said Angelica.

She pulled it out. "I made this clay horse when I was two."

"Let's play horse!" said Chuckie.

"Let's play horse!" said Tommy.

"You be the horse," said Angelica. She jumped on top of Tommy and Chuckie.

"Ride 'em, cowgirl!" yelled Angelica.

Tommy said, "We're not a horse.
We're a bucking bronco."

They bucked Angelica onto the
ground.

Chuckie giggled.

The kids went over to Grandpa.

"There's something flat in this box," said Grandpa.

Grandpa took out a tie. "I gave Stu this tie for his birthday!"

Grandpa took out another tie. "I gave Stu this tie, too."

Grandpa took out another tie. "I gave Stu this tie, too."

Grandpa took out another tie. "And I gave Stu this tie, too. Why, that ungrateful . . . "

17

Tommy, Chuckie, and Angelica were playing a game with the ties. The game was tug-of-war. "Hey, kids, great idea!" said Grandpa. "Let me play, too!"

"Whoa, Nelly!" said Grandpa. "I won!"

Angelica reached into another box. "There's something stretchy in this box," said Angelica. "Oh, yes. These are baby stretchers. Your mom puts them on you when you sleep so you'll grow big and tall."

Tommy said, "There's no such thing as baby stretchers. No way!"

"YES way," said Angelica.

"Let's ask Grandpa," said Tommy.

Tommy gave the baby stretchers to Grandpa.

"Well, I'll be! My old red suspenders," he said. "I wore these when I was a fireman."

Grandpa put the suspenders on. "These remind me of a riddle. Why does a fireman wear red suspenders?"

Grandpa answered his own riddle. "To keep his pants up! Ha! Ha! Ha! Ha! Get it?"

The babies did not get the joke. "Oh, never mind," said Grandpa.

It was time for the sale to begin.
People came to look at the junk.

A man bought the tummy tickler.

"Don't take our tummy tickler!"
cried Chuckie.

A lady bought the baseball pajamas.

"Don't take our baseball pajamas!"
cried Tommy.

A kid bought the clay horse.

"Don't take my clay horse!" cried Angelica.

A man bought the box of ties.

"Don't take our box of ties!" cried Grandpa.

A fireman bought the red suspenders.

"Don't take my red suspenders!" cried Grandpa.

"They took all our junk!" cried
Chuckie. "Waaaaa!"

"And it's hot!" cried Angelica.
"Waaaaa!"

"Let's crawl under this table. It's cooler
in the shade," said Tommy.

A man bought the table. The babies
were hot again.

"Waaaaa!" they all cried.

Then the babies heard something.
DING DING DING!
The babies saw something. MMMMM!
The babies ate something! YUM, YUM!

Tommy's dad used the money from the junk sale to buy ice cream for everyone!

Then Tommy's dad saw something. "Hey, look! The neighbors are having a junk sale, too."

Tommy bought a big umbrella! The babies crawled under it.

The grown-ups cried, "More junk. Oh, no!"

"More junk!" said the babies. "Oh, yes!"